R0064980092

Maddox, Jake.

J
MADDOX   Pit crew crunch

DUE DATE   **MCN**   05/14   23.99

PIT CREW

CRUNCH

BY JAKE MADDOX

illustrated by Sean Tiffany

text by Lisa Trumbauer

STONE ARCH BOOKS
www.stonearchbooks.com

Jake Maddox Books are published by Stone Arch Books
1710 Roe Crest Drive
North Mankato, Minnesota 56003
www.capstonepub.com

Library of Congress Cataloging-in-Publication Data
Maddox, Jake.
    Pit crew crunch / by Jake Maddox; text by Lisa Trumbauer;
    illustrated by Sean Tiffany.
    p. cm. — (Impact books. A Jake Maddox sports story
(on the speedway))
    ISBN 978-1-4342-1600-7
    [1. Stock car racing—Fiction. 2. Automobile racing—Fiction.]
I. Trumbauer, Lisa, 1963– II. Tiffany, Sean, ill. III. Title.
PZ7.M25643Pit 2010
[Fic]—dc22   2009004226

Creative Director: Heather Kindseth
Graphic Designer: Hilary Wacholz

Printed in the United States of America, North Mankato, Minnesota.
042013   007248R

TABLE OF CONTENTS

CHAPTER 1

THE CONTEST

As soon as he got home from school, Peter ran to the mailbox. He flipped open the white metal lid and carefully slid out the mail.

Nothing. Still no letter from the NASCAR officials.

While flipping through a magazine the month before, Peter had seen an interesting ad. The ad announced a new NASCAR contest.

The winner would be able to work on a pit crew for one of the major race car drivers of NASCAR! All Peter had to do was write a short essay, fill out some information, and send in his entry.

Peter couldn't believe his luck. He loved NASCAR more than anything. Winning the contest would be a dream come true.

He knew a lot of kids would enter. But he figured he had a good chance anyway, since he loved NASCAR so much.

He'd given it his best try. He had filled out the form right away and sent it in that very same day.

I think NASCAR is the best sport around! Peter had written. *You have to know how to handle a car. You have to understand engines, tires, and tracks.*

NASCAR is more than just knowing the rules. It's about knowing the mechanics of cars and racing, too.

With my love for cars and racing, I think I'd be an excellent member of any pit crew.

It wasn't hard to explain why he loved NASCAR. The hard part was waiting to find out if he'd won. What was taking the selection committee so long to make a decision?

Peter headed back to the house. He kicked the gravel on the driveway.

He'd been so certain that the notice would come today. After all, it had been almost a month since he sent in the form.

As he walked up the front steps of his house, he heard the phone ring. Peter ran inside and answered it.

"Is this Mr. Peter Granger?" asked a man's voice.

Peter clutched the receiver. "Um, yes. Yes, it is!" he said.

"Mr. Granger, this is Lee Harlow at NASCAR headquarters," the man said. "We are pleased to announce that your contest entry was one of only a few chosen out of several thousands."

Peter gulped. "It was?" he asked.

"Yes!" Mr. Harlow said. "You may be able to work in a pit crew during a NASCAR race!"

CHAPTER 2

TESTS

Peter couldn't believe it. He'd actually won the contest! "This is awesome!" he told Mr. Harlow.

"I'm sorry it took us so long to call you and tell you that you'd won," Mr. Harlow said. "I hope it was worth the wait!"

"It definitely was!" Peter said.

"Good. I'll be sending you some forms to sign. I'll also send you some information about NASCAR," Mr. Harlow said.

"Information?" Peter repeated. "But I already know pretty much everything about NASCAR."

"Yes, but there are rules about working in the pit crew," Mr. Harlow explained. "We can't just let anyone behind the scenes of a NASCAR race. You'll have to pass a few tests before you can help out."

Peter hadn't thought of that. "So it will be a while before I'll actually work the pit crew," he said.

"Not too long," Mr. Harlow said. "Take a look at the information I'm sending and see what you think."

Peter didn't need to look at the information to decide. He knew he'd do whatever it took to be able to work on the pit crew.

He'd dreamed of being part of a NASCAR race for his whole life. He wasn't going to blow this chance.

After Peter hung up the phone, he called his best friend, Kurt. Kurt was just as excited about the pit crew spot as Peter. Peter told him everything Mr. Harlow had said.

"What do you think the tests will be about?" Kurt asked.

"I have no idea, but I'm sure I can pass them, whatever they are," Peter said. "Will you help me out?"

"Of course," said Kurt. "But I don't think you need to worry. You know more about NASCAR than anybody, except maybe your dad. You'll definitely pass the tests."

* * *

Another week went by. Peter checked the mail every day. Finally, there was a thick envelope from Mr. Harlow inside the mailbox.

The envelope contained some forms for Peter and his dad to sign. Mr. Harlow had also sent a lot of information about NASCAR and about working on a pit crew. Peter read all of the information really carefully.

The biggest problem Peter knew he had was that he'd never worked on a real car before. The pit crew preferred members who were experienced. Working on the crew was not easy.

Peter knew it would take practice and hard work. He wasn't afraid of that. He was just worried that he didn't have the right skills to join the crew.

He'd won the contest, but that didn't guarantee him a spot in the pit crew. He hadn't realized when he entered the NASCAR contest that he'd have to pass so many tests.

"I wonder how many more kids have been chosen," Peter said to Kurt.

"Why don't you call Mr. Harlow," Kurt suggested. "I bet he could tell you."

"That's a great idea!" Peter said. He found Mr. Harlow's phone number and called him up.

Mr. Harlow answered the phone right away. He told Peter that four other people had been chosen as possible candidates for joining the pit crew. They all needed to go to the racetrack in two weeks to take the tests.

"I really want the spot, Mr. Harlow," Peter said.

"I like your eagerness, Peter. Just be prepared when you come to the racetrack," Mr. Harlow told him. "We'll see then if you've got what it takes."

CHAPTER 3

HELP
FROM DAD

On Sunday, Peter and his dad planned to watch a NASCAR race together. Peter loved watching the races and hanging out with his dad. It would be the perfect time to tell his dad about the contest.

Just before the race began, Peter brought all of the information from Mr. Harlow into the TV room. His father was sitting down with a bowl of chips and a soda, getting ready to watch the race.

"Hey, Dad, look at this," said Peter. He handed his father a copy of the essay he'd written about NASCAR.

"Is this for school?" Dad asked.

"No," said Peter. "It's for NASCAR."

"NASCAR?" his dad repeated. He frowned and read the essay.

Peter explained how he had entered the contest. "Four other people won, besides me," he said. "Now I have to pass a test to be on the pit crew. So what do you think, Dad?"

"Well, I'm not sure," his father said.

Peter took a deep breath. He remembered what Mr. Harlow had said on the phone. Peter needed to show that he could be a great pit crew member.

"I was wondering if maybe you could help me," Peter said. "I need to learn how to change tires and jack up the car. And maybe you could show me how to quickly screw in the lug nuts and stuff."

"So if you pass the tests, then you get to join the NASCAR pit crew?" his father asked.

"That's what Mr. Harlow told me," Peter said. "He said to meet him next Saturday at the track here in town."

Peter's dad was silent for a moment. The only sound in the room came from the NASCAR announcer on the TV.

Finally, Dad said, "It sounds like a great opportunity."

Peter was once again afraid to breathe. "And?" he said.

"And I think you should definitely go for it," his father said.

"All right!" Peter said. He pumped the air with his fist.

"This is going to be a lot of hard work," his father said. "None of it is going to be easy."

"I'm ready for it!" Peter said. "I feel like I've been ready my entire life!"

"Okay then," his father said. "Let's take notes during this race. Then we'll go out to the garage. We'll see what you can learn on my car."

Then Peter and his father watched the NASCAR race. Together, they paid close attention to the pit crew. In fact, they watched the pit crew more than they watched the cars!

They looked at the second hand on the wall clock in the TV room. They timed how long the pit crew took to change tires, tighten nuts, and jack up the car to look for damage. It only took the crew a few seconds to do all of that work.

Peter felt nervous, watching the pit crew fly through their tasks. How could he ever work that fast?

That week, with his father's help, Peter learned how to change a flat tire. His father timed him as Peter jacked up the car and loosened the lug nuts.

They went to the gas station. There, they timed how quickly Peter could inflate tires.

By the end of the week, Peter felt like he was ready. He was ready to face his competition.

* * *

On Saturday, Dad and Kurt went to the track with him.

When they arrived, Peter looked around. Some other guys were there, talking about the contest.

Peter guessed that they were the other NASCAR fans who had won the essay contest. He hadn't expected all of the other guys to be so much older. They were also a lot bigger.

Peter felt like a little kid compared to the other guys. His confidence drained away.

CHAPTER 4

NOT SO BAD

"Peter, did this contest have an age requirement?" Peter's dad asked.

"It said thirteen and up," Peter said. "I thought a lot of other thirteen-year-old guys like me would enter too."

"Do you recognize any of these guys?" Dad asked.

Peter shrugged. "No. They must be in high school," he said.

"In what grade? Fifteenth?" Dad joked.

"I'm sure they haven't practiced as much as you have," Kurt said. "You've been working really hard. You don't have anything to worry about."

"I hope you're right," Peter said nervously.

Just then, a man in a denim jacket and jeans walked over. "You must be Peter Granger," the man said.

"And you must be Mr. Harlow," Peter said. He stuck out his hand, and Mr. Harlow shook it. "It's nice to meet you," Peter added.

"The pleasure is mine," Mr. Harlow said, smiling. "I'm always glad to meet NASCAR fans. Now, let's get started! Come on over here."

Peter's dad and Kurt went to watch from the stands. Peter and the other contest winners introduced themselves.

Peter had been right. The other guys were all in high school. He was the youngest guy there.

"The first thing you'll have you do is take a written test," Mr. Harlow said.

Some of the older guys groaned. Mr. Harlow chuckled. "Don't worry, guys, this isn't like school," he said. "This will help us figure out how much you know about NASCAR and about racing."

Peter and the other four essay contest winners spread out in the bleachers to take the test. It wasn't the most comfortable place to take a test, but it sure beat sitting in a classroom.

Peter hadn't been expecting a written test. Still, the test was pretty easy. There wasn't a single question he couldn't answer.

Peter knew that NASCAR had started from old bootleggers in the south. He knew that NASCAR stood for the National Association for Stock Car Auto Racing.

He also knew that the start of the NASCAR season actually began with the Daytona 500 in Daytona Beach, Florida. He would bet that a lot of people didn't know that.

Most people would probably assume that the racing season was like the football season. They might figure that the Daytona 500 was kind of like the Super Bowl. But Peter knew that it was held at the beginning of the racing season, not at the end.

Twenty minutes later, Peter handed in his test. He was the first one done. He knew so much about NASCAR that he was sure that he could have answered even more questions.

While he waited for the other guys to finish their tests, he sat back, nervously tapping his feet.

He wanted to show those guys that he could work in a pit crew. He wanted to show them how quick he could be and how strong he was.

He might have been smaller and younger than the other guys, but he was ready for the challenge. He knew he could do it.

Soon, all the tests had been collected. It was time for the next trial.

Mr. Harlow assigned each contestant a number. Peter was given the number 3. For the next challenge, they had to pay attention to five race cars zooming around the track.

When the contestant's numbered car pulled into the stop, the contestant was supposed to hop over the wall and assist. The contestant would take his instructions from the pit crew already there.

Only seven people were allowed to work "over the wall." That was the spot where the race car slowed down and stopped for servicing.

The pit crew was responsible for refueling the car, and for putting air in the tires and changing them if needed. The pit crew also had to recognize any damage and fix it, if possible.

Sometimes the pit crew also helped the driver by making sure he had water to drink.

All these tasks took time, but the pit crew had to work very quickly. They only had fifteen seconds. After that, the car had to start moving again.

Peter waited behind the wall. He watched as the cars zipped along. He looked at the number 3 car.

Finally, the number 3 car was slowing down! Now was his chance!

Peter flung himself over the wall.

CHAPTER 5

SHOW YOUR STUFF

Peter couldn't believe he was standing next to an actual race car. Oh, sure, it probably wasn't like the official cars that had to pass qualifying races to enter a big NASCAR race. But he was as close as he had ever gotten to one!

Peter was surprised when one of the pit crew members threw him a helmet and a pair of gloves.

"Safety first!" the guy said.

Peter jammed everything on as quickly as possible. *Am I being timed for getting dressed, too?* he wondered nervously.

Then he flew into action. Before he knew it, he was pumping air into tires. He was washing windshields. He was helping to secure lug nuts.

Peter could feel the blood rushing through his veins. His hands didn't shake at all as they handled the equipment.

The equipment wasn't exactly like what he'd practiced on at home. How could it be? He'd practiced on a normal car, and this was a race car. But the equipment still felt right in his hands.

Peter's hands seemed to move all on their own. It was like he'd been working in a pit crew forever.

He loved every minute of it — from the smell of the oil and grease to the feel of the warmth of the race car. The six other crew members did their jobs quickly. Everything worked together perfectly, down to the last lug nut.

Soon, the car was once again ready to roll. Peter was tired, but thrilled. Working on the race car had been one of the best moments of his life.

As he stood there, catching his breath, Peter watched the number 3 car ease down the track. The car slowed and stopped.

Busy in the pit crew, Peter hadn't noticed the car's driver. Peter had been too focused on the car. Now he watched as a familiar form emerged.

It was Jimmy Turner.

Jimmy Turner was a master race car driver. He had won several Daytona 500 races. He even starred in a few TV commercials. Jimmy Turner was a king of the racetrack. And he was one of Peter's biggest idols.

Jimmy Turner waved at Peter. "Come on over!" he called.

Peter's hands began to sweat. He placed his gloves and helmet on the wall. Then he walked over to Jimmy.

"Good going, kid!" Jimmy said. "Was that really your first pit crew?"

Peter gulped. "Um, yes. I mean, I practiced with my dad in our garage," he added.

Jimmy laughed. "In your garage?" he asked.

"That's right," Peter said. "But it doesn't really prepare you for the real thing."

"Not exactly," Jimmy said. "Even so, I think you did a fine job."

"Really?" Peter asked. He smiled.

"I'll talk to Mr. Harlow, but I'd like to have you on my crew at least once this year," Jimmy told him. "What do you say?"

"What do I say?" Peter said. What could he say? "I'd love it!"

CHAPTER 6

HARDER
THAN BEFORE

Peter brought Jimmy over to meet his dad and Kurt. Peter's father reached out to shake hands with the race car driver.

"It's a pleasure to meet you," Dad said. "Peter and I have spent many hours watching you race."

"Thanks," Jimmy said, smiling. "It was a pleasure to have your son on my crew today."

"He's a hard worker," Dad said.

"Mr. Turner asked me to work on his pit crew," Peter told his dad.

Jimmy nodded. "Your son did a great job today," he said, "but we still have a ways to go."

"You mean another test?" asked Peter.

"Well, we don't let just anyone work in the pit crew," Jimmy explained. "Besides passing timed tests, each person has to get along with the rest of the crew. And they have to be very hard workers."

Jimmy paused. Then he went on, "The job isn't easy. Lots of people work hard to get here."

"I know Peter would work hard, like everyone else," Dad said.

Jimmy nodded. "He's already shown that he has the ability," he said. "Now we have to see how well he'll be able to work with the team."

Jimmy arranged for Peter to work with the pit crew for the next few Saturdays. Saturday races were usually qualifying races for the drivers. The big events were held on Sundays.

Peter looked forward to every weekend. He loved the rush of the race cars zooming by. He loved the way the crew worked together so the car ran smoothly.

Peter wasn't allowed to work over the wall during the races. But he still helped the pit crew. Instead of jumping over the wall, he'd stand on top of it. That way, he could pass down supplies that the race car driver and the crew needed.

Peter quickly became part of the team. One of the jobs he always did was wiping down the tires. The tires needed to be cleaned off when they got covered in too much gunk. From his perch on the wall, Peter reached down with a long-handled broom. He brushed the gunk off the tires.

He was also a big help to the driver. He found a bucket and attached it to a broom handle. He filled the bucket with water bottles.

From the wall, Peter reached the bucket toward Jimmy. Then all Jimmy had to do was lean over and grab the bottles.

The heat, the noise, the crowd! Peter loved it. He didn't think there was any better place to spend a Saturday than a busy racetrack.

Then one Saturday, Jimmy walked over to Peter after the race.

"Peter, can you work the pit crew tomorrow?" Jimmy asked.

Peter's mouth dropped open. He couldn't believe it. "Seriously?" he asked. "During the real race?"

Jimmy nodded. "I think you're ready," he said. "Now, let's go find you a pit crew suit."

CHAPTER 7

THE WALL

Peter could barely sleep that night. He was too busy thinking about brushing tires and tightening lug nuts.

He got to the track early on Sunday morning. His dad and Kurt headed into the bleachers to watch the race.

Because of Peter's age and his size, he still wasn't allowed to work over the wall. He'd be working on the wall, like he did during the qualifying races.

He was disappointed. At the same time, he also knew he was as close as he'd possibly get to a real NASCAR race.

As Peter slipped his safety suit on, Jimmy walked up.

"The race is about to start," Jimmy said. "Do you think you're ready for your big debut?"

"Yes, sir. I wish I could work over the wall with the pit crew," Peter said. "But I know I'm safer on the wall."

"No one's ever put someone your age over the wall before," Jimmy explained. "So let's see how you do on the wall first."

"Okay," Peter said. "Good luck out there today!"

Jimmy walked away. Then Peter started setting up.

He got his tools ready for the race. His giant broom was ready to wipe down the tires. The bucket was full of water bottles to pass to the driver.

Soon, the race was about to begin. The crowd was getting louder and rowdier.

Peter climbed onto the pit crew wall. He dangled his feet over the side. Within seconds, the race began.

Peter kicked his heels against the pit crew wall as he watched the race. The cars zoomed around the track.

He kept his eyes on Jimmy's green and white car, the one with number 3 painted on the side in black paint. All of a sudden, the car quickly edged out of the pack of dozens of cars.

Jimmy Turner was making a move!

Peter held his breath. In the audience, people started pointing to Jimmy Turner's race car.

Peter checked his watch. He glanced at the giant wall clock near the pit crew station.

It was almost time for Jimmy Turner to pull over. His tires needed air and rubbing down. Parts had to be checked.

And Jimmy was probably hot — really hot — inside his race car. Peter knew that the temperature inside a race car could be more than 100 degrees. Jimmy would need a drink of cold water as soon as he pulled into the pit.

Peter watched as the green and white car slowed down. It neared the pit. It slid to a stop behind the wall.

Peter got ready to stand up. He was prepared.

The first thing he'd do would be to lean over and run his broom across the surface of the car's dirty tires.

Peter started to get to his feet. Then, suddenly, everything went wrong.

CHAPTER 8

CAR HOODS

In all the weeks Peter had worked with the pit crew, he'd never seen a car leave the track and drive into the wall. The movement was completely unexpected.

One minute, Peter had been standing on the wall. The next moment, the wall shook and he was airborne.

Then his feet slammed into the hood of the race car.

Peter's entire body seemed to jostle and grind. The race car shook like crazy beneath him.

Somehow, Peter still managed to hold onto the broom and the bottle of ice water. He didn't drop anything.

Jimmy flung himself out of the car. "What do you think you're doing?" he shouted up at Peter.

Peter felt like he'd been punched in the gut. He'd hit the car really hard. He couldn't seem to find his breath.

"I fell," Peter said.

"That's pretty obvious," Jimmy said.

The pit crew had gone into emergency mode. Peter's father came jogging up. Kurt was right behind him. They had prime seats in the infield.

Dad and Kurt had seen everything —
from Peter climbing the wall to Peter nearly
getting crushed by the race car. Dad looked
really worried.

Peter was glad he was wearing the safety
suit. If it hadn't been for all of the extra
padding, he was sure his body would be in
a million pieces.

"I hope I didn't smash up the car too
much," he said to Mark, the head of the
pit crew.

"Let's get you up off that hood and see
what damage was done — to you and the
car," Mark replied. "With luck, both of you
will be okay. That was quite the fall you
just took."

Dad reached out his hands. He helped
Peter get off the hood.

Peter turned to look at the car. The hood still seemed sturdy. There weren't any dents or bumps or cracks. That was good news.

Peter's back hurt, but the car was fine. But Jimmy still looked upset. His face was red, and he wouldn't look at Peter.

Suddenly, a stretcher appeared at the side of the race car. Peter heard a cheer go up in the grandstands and in the infield. He realized that the audience was cheering for him. They were cheering because Peter was able to move.

Peter let his father and Kurt help him onto the stretcher. Peter was afraid to look at the pit crew. He was mostly afraid to look at Jimmy. They had all put so much faith in him, despite his age and his size. He knew he had let them down.

Peter leaned back on the stretcher. He watched as the scenery changed overhead. Two ambulance drivers lifted him into the ambulance. Peter listened as the cheering and whistling continued.

Then the ambulance doors slammed shut. Everything was quiet as he rode to the hospital.

CHAPTER 9

IN THE HOSPITAL

Dad and Kurt met the ambulance at the hospital. After the ambulance drivers rolled Peter into the building, Dad leaned over to give him a hug. Then he thought better of it. Peter was all banged up, after all. A hug would hurt him more than help.

Even the ride on the stretcher was painful. The stretcher bounced along the winding hospital halls.

Peter was sure he'd need X-rays or something. The doctors would have to make sure he hadn't broken anything too seriously.

Peter wiggled his arms and legs. Everything seemed to be working. Sweat began to bead on his forehead. He was starting to feel uncomfortable and hot in his safety suit.

The ambulance drivers wheeled Peter into the emergency room. They brought him to an empty bed.

Peter watched as Dad pulled the privacy curtain around his bed. There was a small TV nearby, tuned to the NASCAR race.

"I still don't understand how you managed to get yourself knocked off the wall," Dad said.

Peter wanted to shrug, but it hurt too much. The pain was getting to be unbearable.

"I guess a real race is way different from working the crew at a practice race," Peter said. "I should have practiced falling," he added.

Just then, a bunch of doctors and nurses marched over to Peter's bed. One of the doctors slid a heartbeat monitor over Peter's arm.

The other doctors took his temperature and checked his blood pressure. Everything seemed normal.

"I think you just need to rest," one of the nurses said. "And we'll get you out of this suit and into something a little more comfortable."

Peter actually wanted to keep wearing his safety suit. As long as he had it on, he still felt like he was part of the pit crew.

If he changed into the hospital clothes, he'd have to admit that he'd messed up. He'd let Jimmy down.

Just then, the privacy curtain was pushed aside. Peter couldn't believe it when he saw the familiar face. Jimmy Turner walked up to his bed.

"What are you doing here?" Peter asked, shocked. "Shouldn't you be finishing up the race right now?"

"I had to make sure you were okay," Jimmy explained. "I can't let a member of my team go to the hospital without checking on them," he added. "I was worried about you."

Peter looked away from Jimmy. "I guess I'm not part of the team anymore," Peter said sadly. "After what happened today, I mean."

Jimmy frowned. "Who says? It's my decision who works on my team," he told Peter. "Now that we both know what to expect, we'll be more careful. You'll wear more safety gear, for one thing. And we'll keep you behind the wall. You'll get special equipment so you can still help out, but you'll be safer that way. I don't want to lose one of the hardest-working members of my team."

"Really?" Peter asked happily. "I can keep working on the crew?" He looked over at his dad.

"If we can make sure you're safe, I don't see a problem," Dad said.

Peter smiled. "Yes!" he said. "We can go over all the safety stuff before I work another race."

"Speaking of races, today's is only half over," Jimmy said. "Let's watch the rest. Let's see which bucket of bolts actually wins!"

Peter laughed. The pain he'd felt almost disappeared. He and Jimmy sat back and watched the rest of the race.

ABOUT THE AUTHOR

Lisa Trumbauer was the *New York Times* best-selling author of *A Practical Guide to Dragons*. In addition, she wrote about 300 other books for children, including mystery novels, picture books, and nonfiction books on just about every topic under the sun (including the sun!).

ABOUT THE ILLUSTRATOR

When Sean Tiffany was growing up, he lived on a small island off the coast of Maine. Every day, from sixth grade until he graduated from high school, he had to take a boat to get to school. When Sean isn't working on his art, he works on a multimedia project called "OilCan Drive," which combines music and art. He has a pet cactus named Jim.

GLOSSARY

committee (kuh-MIT-ee)—a group of people who discuss things and make decisions for a larger group

competition (kom-puh-TISH-uhn)—a person you are trying to beat in a contest

confidence (KON-fuh-dents)—a strong belief in a person's abilities

contestant (kon-TES-tent)—a person who takes part in a contest

experienced (ek-SPIHR-ee-uhnst)— made skillful from the practice of doing something

guarantee (gair-uhn-TEE)—a promise that something will definitely happen

mechanics (muh-KAN-iks)—related to machines

WHO'S WHO IN THE
PIT CREW

A pit crew consists of a jackman, two tire changers, two tire carriers, a gasman, and a catch can man. Here's a look at who does what.

During tire changes, the **jackman** lifts one side of the car with a hydraulic jack for tire changes. After the first side is changed, the jackman must hurry around to the other side, carrying the 35-pound jack. He then jacks up that side.

The **tire changers** use an airgun to loosen and tighten the lug nuts that hold on the tires. There is a changer for the front tires and one for the rear tires.

The **tire carriers** help the changers. They carry 75-pound tires from behind the wall and put them on the car. The changers can then tighten the lug nuts.

The **gasman** is responsible for filling the car's fuel cell. He hoists a 80-pound gas can up to the car to fill the cell. One or two gas cans are used per pit stop, depending on how much fuel is needed.

The **catch can man** catches fuel when the tank is full. The catch can is shaped like a box. It has a valve that plugs in to the back of the car. When the tank is full, extra fuel flows out the valve and into the catch can. Then, the catch can man waves to let the driver know that the fuel cell is full.

DISCUSSION QUESTIONS

1. How do you think Peter felt when he saw the other boys he had to compete against for a spot on the pit crew?

2. Why do you think the contest included a written exam? Why was it important for the contestants to know so much about NASCAR?

3. Do you think it was a good decision for Jimmy to leave the race at the end of the book?

WRITING PROMPTS

1. Peter worked hard to earn a spot on the pit crew. Have you ever worked hard to achieve a goal? Write about your experience.

2. Have you ever injured yourself while participating in a sport or activity? Write about it.

3. Reread the first two pages of chapter seven. Think about what Jimmy was seeing from inside the car. Now rewrite the scene from his point of view.